Wireless

Mysteries

Old Testament

By Michael Yates

Nettle Books

Published 2016 by Nettle Books
nettlebooks@hotmail.co.uk

ISBN: 978-0-9933729-0-2

Classification: Drama

This volume is dedicated to our Patron
Mary Creagh, MP for Wakefield;
and also to our Director
Howard Frost
whose tragic death meant a final halt to our
CD ambitions.

The cast of a proposed Wakefield Wireless Mysteries CD was: COLIN ATKINSON as God, COLIN BEAL as Esau, HOWARD FROST as Abraham, John Milton; JEET GANGULY as Pharaoh; SHREE GANGULY as Hagar; PENNY GRAY as Continuity Announcer; JULIE GREENWOOD as Sarah; ALEXANDER GRIEVE as Abel; STEFAN GRIEVE as Adam, Noah; PAUL HALEY as King of Babylon, Satan, Archangel Gabriel; LOUIS KASATKIN as Cain, Jacob; ANN LUMB as Isaac; KATE MEHTA as Headline Announcer, Angel; DIANE PEEL as Eve; JOSIE WALSH as Noah's Neighbour; MICHAEL YATES as Jim Everyman, Ham, Archangel Michael.

In September 2014, the play was performed live at the Orangery in Wakefield as part of the Wakefield Literary Festival with a grant from that organisation. The cast for this performance differed because some of the CD actors were not available. The live cast was: COLIN BEAL as Abel; HOWARD FROST as Abraham, John Milton; JEET GANGULY as Pharaoh; SHREE GANGULY as Hagar; STEFAN GRIEVE as Adam, Noah; PAUL HALEY as King of Babylon, Satan, Archangel Gabriel; LOUIS KASATKIN as Cain; BENJAMIN LANE as Isaac; ANN LUMB as Continuity Announcer; KATE MEHTA as Sarah, Angel; DIANE PEEL as Eve, Headline Announcer; JOSIE WALSH as Noah's Neighbour; MATT YATES as God; MICHAEL YATES as Jim Everyman, Ham, Archangel Michael.

For both the CD and the live performances, Director: HOWARD FROST; Producer: LOUIS KASATKIN. For the CD, Sound engineer and Musical Director: MATT YATES

Wireless Mysteries
Old Testament

This volume cannot pretend to be an actual translation of the Wakefield Mystery Plays, the literary heritage of my home city, performed in its medieval streets. But in terms of content, my play follows the original: The War in Heaven, the Creation, the Fall, Cain and Abel, Noah and the Flood, Abraham, Jacob and Esau.

When I decided to write a modern version, I knew I could never be Cecil B DeMille or Ridley Scott. No massive crowd scenes, no huge cast of actors, no CGI. So I decided to write an audio version, with a small group of actors playing many parts. And I have presented the material as a parody of radio news and drama: the studio debate; the daily soap opera, a bit like *The Archers*; the one-off crime drama; and what used to be called the fireside chat, in this case with God himself.

Like the Medieval originals, the play is a mixture of sacred and profane. The humour is broad with a touch of pantomime, which struck me as the closest you could get in modern drama to the mind-set of the Mysteries.

I chose to write my dialogue in modern prose rather than the rhyming verse of the originals. The one exception is the Good Angels who talk in regular metre and rhyme because they "fit in": they are contented puppets within their happy world.

For my purposes, God speaks like a blunt Yorkshireman. He's working class (he is, after all, the bricklayer who built the universe), down-to-earth, one of the lads, generous, but flares up when betrayed. He's intimate and affable when addressing the radio audience direct; but, like any good politician, he also has a more formal style, as when addressing the Angelic Host. Satan is a pantomime demon king and I wanted his Devils to sound like Daleks.

I've humanised the Biblical characters by emphasising their downside now and again: Abraham is often cowardly and unprincipled (which befits a man who will trade his wife to Pharaoh pretending she's his sister); Noah likes his drink; Jacob is on the make (as befits a man who will submit to 14 years servitude to get on in life).

But beneath all this, I like to think that, like its famous ancestors, it's a serious work. The recurring theme is obligation: of sons to fathers (God and Adam, Abraham and Isaac, Noah and Ham); of husbands to wives (Abraham and Sarah, Abraham and Hagar); of brother to brother (Cain and Abel, Isaac and Ishmael, Jacob and Esau); of God to Man and Man to God.

And the recurring images include sacrifice (the burnt offerings of Abraham, plus the "real" sacrifices of Adam sharing Eve's apple, knowing death lies ahead, and Abraham willing to sacrifice his son Isaac, presaging the story of Jesus). Then there are the knives (Abraham hiding first his circumcising blade then his sacrificial dagger; Cain producing his murder weapon).

As in all good stories, character and incident are everything.

Michael Yates 2016

Wireless Mysteries:
Old Testament

RADIO JINGLE MUSIC

VOICES:

Start the day right
With the station that's bright.
Kick out the dark
And let in the light!
With...
Radio Universe!

PAUSE, THEN...

ANNOUNCER: And now for today's episode of At Home with the Nomads, an everyday story of desert folk. Abraham and his wife Sarah are getting ready for a well-earned retirement. But there are still some surprises in store.

SOAP OPERA THEME MUSIC

ABRAHAM: Abraham's Diary, 21st of April 5,000 BC. (PAUSE) God knows, I've never been an adventurous sort of man. I was never really cut out for the life of a nomad, so I was very pleased when Sarah and I found this nice little space for the caravan. There's a bit of shade, enough room to pitch a good size tent and a perfectly adequate watering hole for the camels. Then this morning something happened...

7

FADE DOWN, FADE UP

SARAH: I know you always wanted a child, Abraham, a son to follow you in the great nomadic tradition. I know that's why you married me. Because I was much younger and you thought I'd be fruitful. But I'm barren. And we have to face up to that.

ABRAHAM: Don't worry, Sarah. (BEAT) Anyway, children are always a problem. If we did have a son, what would we leave him? A tent and a few camels isn't much these days. (SIGH) I guess I'm not much of a nomad at all. I've got no get-up-and-go.

SARAH: You're a good man, Abraham, and you've always followed God's ways. (BEAT) Don't worry about being such an old stick-in-the mud. I like the quiet life myself.

ABRAHAM: Well, what's the life of a nomad all about? Travel, travel, put down tent pegs, pull them up again, move on. Maybe now's the time to settle down once and for all.

SARAH: Yes, I think maybe it is.

THUNDERCLAP

SARAH: Oh God! What's happening?

ABRAHAM: It *is* God! I'd know that clap of thunder anywhere!

GOD: Good man, Abraham. You've got it right, lad. It *is* God. I was in these parts anyway and I thought I'd drop in. (BEAT) I know it's a bit theatrical, this thunder, but then

I'm a bit theatrical. No good hiding your light under a bushel if you're God. Now a burning bushel might be different. Eye-catching. (WHISPERED ASIDE) Ay, I must have a look at that some time. (BEAT) Anyway, I've been making plans.

SARAH: Is that good or bad? When God makes plans for people...

GOD: ...you'd better go along with them, Sarah!

SARAH: That's exactly what I was going to say. Whatever you suggest, Lord God, I'm sure we'll enjoy it. In the end.

ABRAHAM: What do you want, Lord? Speak and we obey!

SARAH: But try to be nice to us for once.

GOD: I want you to take a little trip. Bit of an excursion. To Canaan.

SARAH: Canaan? Why Canaan? It's just another piece of desert like this one.

GOD: Nay, it's the Blackpool of the Middle East, lass. Flowing with milk and honey. Or it will be when I've developed it a bit.

SARAH: Milk and honey in the future, but no jam today. I've heard it's very sandy. Just like here. Bit of scrubland maybe. The odd cactus.

ABRAHAM: Actually, Lord, we're very settled here. We were just talking about it...

9

GOD: Settled? Oh come on! I thought you'd be pleased that I've got an opening for you. A new position in life. Opportunities like this don't grow on palm trees. Not at *your* age.

ABRAHAM: What is the job?

SARAH: (INTERRUPTING): He's not the man he used to be. I won't have him lifting heavy things.

ABRAHAM: And I'm not clever any more, either. Set in my ways. I don't fancy going back to college. They'll all be younger than me.

GOD: Oh come on! They'll all be younger than you wherever you go. (BEAT) But it's a simple job, no qualifications needed. No lifting either. All I want you to do is keep my laws…

SARAH: He does that already.

GOD: …and become the father of a great race who will be my chosen people.

SILENCE, THEN SIMULTANEOUSLY…

ABRAHAM: I can't be a father at my age!

SARAH: And I've always been barren!

THEN…

GOD: Well, things are about to change round here!

SOAP OPERA THEME MUSIC, FADE UP, FADE DOWN

ANNOUNCER: In the next episode, Sarah has a controversial suggestion to help Abraham in God's ambitious plan for a chosen people. Tune in tomorrow to find out what it is.

CRACKLING SOUND LIKE AN OLD-FASHIONED RADIO BEING TUNED, THEN:

GOD: Hello listeners. This is God speaking. Really. (BEAT) And you've probably noticed from the way I talk that I'm a Yorkshireman. Well, you always knew God was a Yorkshireman, didn't you? (BEAT) Of course, being God, I'm lots of things to lots of people. But I thought I'd be a Yorkshireman tonight because any Yorkshire people out there would appreciate the thought. And it gives me a chance to be blunt, down-to-earth, call a spade a shovel sort of thing. (BEAT) Now I know people are a bit sceptical these days. They don't think God would bother using something as old-fashioned as steam radio. You probably thought I'd tweet or send an e-mail. But no. I'm an oldee worldee sort of chap. (BEAT) Also, you lot live within time and I don't. And that's another good reason for being a Tyke. I can say *thee* and *tha* now and again. When I remember. Just to remind you I'm timeless. (BEAT) There's a big difference in outlook, let me tell you, when tha lives outside of time. To me, it's not cause and effect, one damn thing after another. It's all one to me, the whole thing, alpha and omega, world without end, forever. But for you lot everything has to have a start. A big bang. So you might think, as you listen here, that some of the scenes you're about to hear are in the wrong order. That such and such couldn't happen until after whatsitsname. But remember: every beginning is also an end. Of something. And here's one coming up now! (VOICE FADES)

THE BONG OF BIG BEN HERALDS THE START OF A
RADIO NEWS PROGRAMME

HEADLINE ANNOUNCER: War in Heaven nearing its end,
say military leaders.

BONG

HEADLINE ANNOUNCER: But where is Satan? Location of
rebel leader remains a mystery.

BONG

HEADLINE ANNOUNCER: United Galaxies Security
Council passes resolution asking that the rights of Fallen
Angels be respected. This is a time for reconciliation with
the Forces of Evil, says United Galaxies General Secretary.

NEWS PROGRAMME MUSIC, THEN:

PRESENTER: Good evening. Welcome to the BBC's
Universal Service. I'm Jim Everyman. (BEAT) Our top
story tonight. Reports from many parts of Heaven have
confirmed that the government of God Almighty is still in
power after what observers have described as the most
significant threat to His rule since the beginning of
Eternity. We are now going over to our religious and
foreign affairs correspondent John Milton at the Gates of
Paradise.

PAUSE, CRACKLE

PRESENTER: I'm sorry. There seems to be a problem with
our line at the moment. Nevertheless here in our studio we
do have His Royal Majesty the King of Babylon, who has

been a vociferous opponent of God for some centuries and has now added his voice to the calls for leniency to the defeated rebels. Welcome to the studio, Your Majesty.

KING OF BABYLON: Thank you, Jim.

PRESENTER: Now, you are an advocate of reconciliation...

KING OF BABYLON: Yes indeed. What has been obvious from the start of this needless conflict is that God must take into account the aspirations of the growing class of educated, liberal-minded angels who supported General Lucifer, or Satan, as we must now call him. And the whole universe is looking for a move to greater democracy and an awareness that right and wrong no longer have absolute meaning in the real world. It's simply no good God telling us he is alpha and omega. What we say is: Come on! There are a lot more than two letters in the Greek alphabet and every letter should have the chance to play its part in a new coalition government. What we say...

PRESENTER: (INTERRUPTING): I'm sorry but (BRIEF CRACKLE) we do seem to have re-established the connection with John Milton. (BEAT) Hello John. The sound isn't brilliant our end but I know you can hear me. And perhaps you can now go ahead and justify the ways of God to man. (BEAT) First of all, what appears to have been the deciding factor in the recent fighting?

JOHN MILTON: Weapons of Mass destruction. Most notably the Angel Michael who spent considerable time in personal combat with the rebel leader and is now, I believe, promoted to Archangel.

13

PRESENTER: A controversial decision, some would say! (BEAT) And what has happened to the rebel leader? We've had contradictory reports...

JOHN MILTON: I have now been reliably informed that *him the Almighty Power hurled headlong, flaming from the ethereal sky with hideous ruin and combustion down to bottomless perdition, there to dwell in adamantine chains and penal fire.*

PRESENTER: One must suppose *that the thought of lost happiness and lasting pain torments him; round he throws his baleful eyes that witnessed huge affliction and dismay mixed with obdurate pride and steadfast hate.*

JOHN MILTON: Yes. That's exactly how I would have put it. Life, Jim, but not as we know it. *At once as far as angels ken he views the dismal situation waste and wild, a dungeon horrible, on all sides round as one great furnace flames, yet from those flames no light, but rather darkness visible serves only to discover sights of woe, regions of sorrow...*

KING OF BABYLON: May I interrupt here? It seems to me that God must have had some foreknowledge of all this. For surely Hell is the sort of place that must have been prepared long ago for these rebels.

PRESENTER: Let me get this straight. You're suggesting that God anticipated the rebellion and therefore has some responsibility for what happened? Some blame in fact?

KING OF BABYLON: And I predict we have not heard the last of the Fallen Angels. I imagine they are planning their next strike even now.

PRESENTER: Guerrilla warfare. Terrorism. (BEAT) Is that what we're likely to see, John?

JOHN MILTON: Oh yes. But I remind you of one thing: If God knew beforehand about the rebellion, he will certainly be able to predict their next atrocity. He will certainly... (VOICE FADES, MORE CRACKLE)

PRESENTER: I'm sorry. We have once again lost the words of John Milton. Well, it seems the conflict may be far from over. And that God is well aware of this...

FADE DOWN, TRUMPETS, FADE UP...

GOD: *Well aware!* I should *say* I was bloody aware! (BEAT) This is God again. And I would like to explain my position. (COUGHS) Right, my policy on angels. First I made them all to be good and obedient and faithful. And I'm a great believer in equal opportunities, so they all looked alike. On the other hand, I like a bit of variety too. So then I made the different kinds: the seraphim, the cherubim and so on. But then I thought: there's summat missing. You know what that was? It was free will. (BEAT) You see, I made the universe not just to be physical but moral as well. So I started giving angels free will, because otherwise there couldn't be a moral universe. And, yes, it's caused a lot of trouble. I don't deny it. (BEAT) There are some people who say: If you're God, you must be omniscient, and if you let bad things happen, it's your fault. Well, I *am* omniscient and I *do* know what's

15

going to happen. But the thing about free will is this: that all of creation – that's all of the angels for a start – are responsible for what they do. And so are you. *All* of you. (BEAT) Anyway, now I've dealt with the angels I've got a whole new project. Mankind. That's you lot. Although I've not made you yet. You might say: Well, if you've not made us yet, what are we doing here? And the answer, as I've told you before, is: *you* exist in time and I do not. (BEAT) Anyway, Mankind. My new project, tha knows. Let's hear how it's all getting along.

FADE, THEN CRACKLE, THEN ETHEREAL MUSIC

ANGEL CHORUS:
O Hail to God Almighty!
All hail! And Brightly!

GOD: I thank you, my loyal angels, my comrades, my good mates in fact. You who have flown by my side on many bold missions. You know I am the first and the last. I am one God in majesty, marvellous and mighty, Father, Son and Holy Ghost, which may never be divided, except in sentences like the one I've just spoken. I am without beginning and without end. And today we stand at the beginning of a new world. I have split the heaven from the earth, the light from the dark, the ocean from the land…

CRASH OF WAVES

GOD: In the waters, the fish will drink and be nourished. Out of the land herbs and plants will spring, trees will flourish and their fruit will succour the myriad creatures who fly, run and crawl. And I have made the days: morning and evening both, the sun to serve daylight and the moon to rule the night. And this is only the fifth day.

ANGEL CHORUS (AMAZED):
All this in five days! Our three-fold God,
all mirth and merriment and good
be sung of you, for your creation
is universal, an eternal sensation!
You have made all that is,
so nothing is amiss,
a world without fault
beneath heaven's vault.
Such is your might
that all is filled with light
though he who was bright
has fallen from the height.
Lucifer we called him, now Satan shall reap
the harvest of his crime, locked away in the Deep.

FADE DOWN, THEN A LONG, LOUD HIDEOUS CRY

SATAN: I, Satan, make my cries but they do not hear me. Shall none then hear me ever? Oh, I think they *shall*! Once I was fair and bright and I did covet the name and state of God. I saw my strength incomprehensible, I wished the Master to call *me* Master, wished God should worship *me*. Now all my following is you, my demons, my fallen angels! And all my hope is you, though hope must never enter where we lie.

DEMON CHORUS: O you monster, prince of dark! In this gloom we see your true light! Once we thought you brighter than bright. But you brought us Hell, you promised false and you delivered damnation! How are we

17

to blame when we were so deceived? Surely God himself is more to blame than us? Yes, yes! For he made us frail and vulnerable to your black thoughts! You and God are to blame for our terrible fall!

SATAN: Oh, this pleases me! Oh, I had thought the hard lesson learned in the battle with God Himself might have moulded you, helped you discover new courage, wrought in you twisted feelings of nobility. Then I would have been lost indeed. But now I see you shrink eternally from knowledge of yourselves and acceptance of your guilt. If you so deny, then I can still mislead and everything is possible. (LAUGHS) I hear God is on the radio today. Even as we speak and weep. We should listen in.

DEMON CHORUS:Spy on him, yes! And so we know what plans he makes, what pains he takes.

SATAN: Pain! Now there is a word fit for all of us. Let us find a way to share our pain!

CRACKLE OF THE RADIO

DEMON CHORUS: (RISING TO A CRESCENDO): Pain! Pain! Pain! Pain! Pain!

CRACKLE OF THE RADIO FADES

MUSIC FADE UP, FADE DOWN

ANNOUNCER: And now for today's episode of At Home with the Nomads, an everyday story of desert folk. Today we find Abraham and Sarah settling down in their new home in Canaan…

18

SOAP OPERA MUSIC FADES UP, FADES DOWN, THEN…

ABRAHAM: Abraham's Diary 23rd of May 4,907 BC. (PAUSE) Well, here we are in Canaan and the weather's quite warm. It's not quite got the views of our last home but it's not bad for people of limited income at our time of life… (VOICE FADES)

SARAH: Well, Abraham, we're here. In Canaan. Have another cup of wine.

ABRAHAM: Yes. I will, Sarah my love. And yes, we're here. In Canaan. We *are*. No doubt about it. That's a relief.

SARAH: But it's not a bit like the brochure. I'm quite disappointed. (BEAT) At least we've got the tent up.

ABRAHAM: Well, you and Hagar got the tent up. I didn't do anything. To be honest, I've never been good at putting up tents.

SARAH: You did lots. You washed the wine cups, fed the camels. I told you I didn't like you lifting things.

ABRAHAM (SIGHS): It's no good. I've been writing my diary, saying nice things about it, trying to look on the bright side, trying to be cheerful. But I can't go on fooling myself. I can't see we've got any future here. I just don't know what God's playing at.

SARAH: Careful. You don't want him hearing you when you say things like that.

ABRAHAM: But he's God. He hears all my words before I say them. Before I even *think* them. That's the trouble. That's what makes me nervous all the time.

SARAH: Never mind. I've got an important question for you. (CLEARS HER THROAT) What do you think about Hagar?

ABRAHAM: Hagar?

SARAH: Our servant girl.

ABRAHAM: Sarah, I *know* who she is. I've not lost my marbles just yet. Look, if you're going to test my memory, it's no good asking me about somebody I see every day. The trick is to ask me the day of the week or what my birthday is or who's the King of Mesopotamia. Or even if I can *spell* Mesopotamia. Which I can't anyway. So don't ask me that.

SARAH: So what do you think of her, Abraham?

ABRAHAM: She's fine. As servant girls go. I mean we've had quite a few. She's a good worker, she's pretty smart, she's got used to the camels very quickly. I've no complaints. Trouble with servant girls is you train them up and get them settled, then they meet some sheikh in the desert and get whisked away.

SARAH: Ah. Well, that's what I wanted to talk about. Whisking.

ABRAHAM: Whisking? What's that mean? Is this another test?

SARAH: Well, maybe not *whisking* exactly. Maybe that's too lively a word. (BEAT) How can I put this? (BEAT) Abraham, God has given us a job. To produce a race of people who will be *his* people. But *I* can't do that.

ABRAHAM: Well, I don't think *I* can either.

SARAH: Oh, I'm sure you can. I'm sure *one* of us can. Otherwise God wouldn't have bothered to ask. No. The problem is me. (BEAT) But I've got a solution…

ABRAHAM: Go on.

SARAH: Well, answer me now. What do you think of Hagar?

ABRAHAM: I've told you!

SARAH: She's nice, isn't she? I mean, you like her, don't you?

ABRAHAM: Well, she's allright.

SARAH: Oh, she's better than allright. She's a looker. She's gorgeous.

ABRAHAM: Yes. OK. She's got a lovely face.

SARAH: And great legs. Did you notice her legs?

ABRAHAM: Sarah, she always wears a baggy dress down to her ankles, which I understand is very fashionable among young people these days. I can't say I've really seen her legs.

21

SARAH: Well, *I* have. And I have to say they're very long and very smooth.

ABRAHAM: OK, I'll take your word for it.

SARAH: And her breasts. They're very ample for a girl of her age. And nicely shaped. Round, but not like footballs. Sensual, I'd call them. God, I remember when I had breasts like that…

ABRAHAM: You still do.

SARAH: Oh, it's nice of you to say so. I feel quite embarrassed.

ABRAHAM: Well, to be honest, Sarah, I'm feeling quite embarrassed myself. Where is this conversation going?

SARAH: All I'm saying is: Those hips! Those thighs! She's probably good at child-bearing. So you can't have a son with me. But with *her*…

ABRAHAM: You mean…

SARAH: Yes. You must father a child with Hagar. You must make her your second wife. It's the only way.

ABRAHAM: But I've never been interested in having a second wife. If I'm honest, she scares me a bit. No, she scares me a lot. It's because she's tall.

SARAH: Oh, everything scares *you*. Tall or short, fat or thin. Makes no difference. But you must think of the future. We must both of us think about the future!

SOAP OPERA MUSIC FADE UP, FADE DOWN

ANNOUNCER: In the next episode, Abraham is pretty annoyed when Sarah has a fling with the Egyptian Pharaoh. But maybe it's *his* fault. And how will Pharaoh react to a very angry God? Tune in tomorrow.

FADE DOWN, FADE UP

GOD: Now beasts, come forth! God calls you!

ROAR OF LIONS, CHATTER OF MONKEYS, SCREAM OF BIRDS

GOD: I see you are good. I see my creation is good. (BEAT) One more thing I will do. I will make Man in my image and he will be keeper of this new world, this earth.

ANGEL CHORUS:
Keeper of great beasts that prowl!
Ranger of sea and air, fish and fowl!
Everything in sky, on water, land
Shall bow to his strong hand.

GOD: O man, O Adam, I give you wit and sense and strength. I give you joy. I give you endless life in Paradise.

THUNDERCLAP

GOD: But it's not good to be alone. Only *I* can be alone and happy with my state, for I am all things anyway. So. While you sleep, young Man, I take your rib...

SOUND OF CRACKING BONE

GOD: And from this rib I make a woman, Eve, who shall be your helper and your friend. Together you shall govern this world, and you shall govern her as I govern you. (BEAT) I mean *thee*.

TRUMPET, THEN:

ADAM: (CRIES OUT): I awake! O Beauty! Wonder! O God, My father...

Eve (CRIES OUT): I too awake! I see as my husband sees! O God...

ADAM: Eve, my wife, you are the most beautiful of all creation! I love you with all my might.

EVE: And Adam, I love you. (WHISPERING ASIDE) But no. How can this be? You did not look upon me first. First you looked upon God. First you called *him* Father. Only then did you speak your love for me. So what is God to me? Merely my husband's father. I do not see as my husband sees. (CRIES OUT) O Adam, this is strange!

ADAM: All is strange when new.

CRACKLE OF RADIO, THEN TRIUMPHANT CRY OF SATAN, THEN

SATAN: Listen to them! Listen! It is a riddle. And I, Satan, know the answer. He has set us up to oppose him. This is his new battle ground, his new arena. It is Man.

DEMON CHORUS: We do not understand.

SATAN: Listen, Demons! That God whom we opposed, there's part of him requires our continuous revolt, eternal intransigence.

DEMON CHORUS: Then how shall we proceed?

SATAN: We shall listen, we shall hear...

CRACKLE OF THE RADIO, THEN:

GOD: Adam and Eve, look about you. Your God commands you. See the herbs and plants and trees. See the creatures that roar and chatter, scream and swoop. Look on the waters where the silver fish swim cunningly. All creatures are your friends. (BEAT) Now, I'm sure you two young people have plenty of things to do. Angels, let's make ourselves scarce and leave them in peace and privacy. (BEAT) Oh, I nearly forgot. A little word in your shell-like. One word only, one word of warning.

ADAM: Speak it, O Lord. I know your word is just.

EVE: Speak it, O father of my husband! For I wish to be convinced.

GOD: (LAUGHS): It's embarrassing really. I don't want to make too much of it. (BEAT) It's only a tree!

ADAM: (UNCOMPREHENDING): A tree?

GOD: See where my finger points. That one over there. By the waterfall. So there can be no doubt. No doubt at all.

THUNDERCLAP

ADAM: Now I see it! I see the tree!

EVE: Oh, it is a handsome tree! And does it have a name?

GOD: It's the Tree of Knowledge, Knowledge of Good and Evil, the only one of its kind. That's why it's very precious to me. Climb it if you want, trim its branches or festoon it with seashells. I don't care. But don't eat the fruit. For then you'll know the taste of Evil. And that would really upset me. And you wouldn't like me when I'm upset.

ADAM: Evil? Is that a bitter taste?

GOD: No, lad, not at first. It's a little bit on the sweet side, if I'm honest, and it's very juicy, and it's very tempting on a hot day.

ADAM: Hah! The heat of the day cannot make me disobey my God.

EVE: But we are newly made and have yet to know how hot the day may well become.

GOD: Now we love you and leave you, my angels and me. But we shall return. Oh yes. (VOICE FADES)

CRACKLE OF RADIO, THEN

SATAN: Listen, fellow demons! He leaves. The holy tyrant leaves.

DEMON CHORUS: He has such confidence in his new creation.

SATAN: No. He offers me my chance.

26

DEMON CHORUS: He knows you listen? He knows Satan listens?

SATAN: He knows I listen. All that I am and ever was and ever shall be, he knows.

DEMON CHORUS: And still you will go?

SATAN: I am as steadfast as He, though I do not know what outcome lies ahead. But yes, I go. I fly. To Earth. To the realm of this upstart Mankind. I am doomed never to leave this damned place, so I will instead carry it with me.

DEMON CHORUS: And bring it to others! And bring it to Mankind! We approve, oh we approve!

RUSHING SOUND LIKE A JET ENGINE, THEN...

SNAKE-CHARMER MUSIC, FAINT BIRDSONG, THEN...

SATAN: Hissss!! Oh what joy to be a serpent! Oh, the belly is the seat of all emotion: hunger, hatred, rage. So I who was Lucifer, I who am Satan, will be a serpent and I will crawl on my belly and I will pretend I look up at all Creation. I will pretend to look up at all Mankind. I will kiss his heel, wind myself around his toes. How little he will reckon me. (BEAT) Here then is Earth, its grasses soft beneath me. Here then is the Tree of Knowledge, forbidden to the tenants of this Paradise, cut off from their feeble imaginings. Except...

EVE: (RAISED VOICE AS IF FROM A DISTANCE): Adam, do not fear. I will not go far. Do not be frightened just because I leave your sight.

27

ADAM: (AS IF FROM A DISTANCE): I do not fear. For what is there to fear? No, but I am unsettled when you are not within my gaze.

EVE: You flatter me to make me best accept your will, your governance.

SATAN: (WHISPERED ASIDE): Will? Governance? What does this woman say? Is this thought of hers not the baby brother of my own rebellion? Is it Eve then whom I should woo? Is it *her* heel I should kiss, her toes I should rub against my mottled skin? Well, well...

FOOTSTEPS GET LOUDER, THEN...

SATAN: (SHOUTING): Take care, O beautiful one! Do not tread so carelessly! Do not crush me who am harmless and a friend!

EVE: (SURPRISED): Serpent! (PAUSE) How is it I know your name yet have never before seen you?

SATAN: Hissss!!! Oh, the greatness of God is that he plants inside of us a friendly vision of all things created so we become straightway on meeting, one family, one tribe, one mind. Is it not so?

EVE: It must be so. I marvel at your wisdom which is yet a small remove from my own, from that of Womankind.

SATAN: Oh no, you flatter me. I am only the Serpent, the servant, the lowly one, the crawler in mud and habitant of holes and crannies. No, no, it is you who hold all wisdom.

EVE: Let us both accept there are things unknown to each of us. For neither of us is God.

SATAN: Hissss!! And why are we not?

EVE: (LAUGHS): Only God is God.

SATAN: And what is it that sets him aside? What knowledge makes him better and higher? Do we not touch the same earth, its shrubs and vegetation? Do we not visit with the animals, blink at the sun and screw up our eyes to glimpse the stars? What truth is hidden from us that we are not also Godlike?

EVE: I do not know. Unless…

SATAN: Unless…?

EVE: There is one thing. One thing forbidden. One limitation.

SATAN: Hissss!! One thing forbidden. One limitation. Such an idea I can scarcely credit. For is not God the most generous, benevolent, loving… ?

EVE: Oh yes, oh yes.

SATAN: And yet he forbids! How can such a one forbid? And what is it he dares to put beyond the wisdom of Womankind?

EVE: It is a fruit. A tree. There. You see?

SATAN: I see you point that dainty finger, O Beautiful One. Yet I see nothing to warrant anguish. I see only trees. I raise my head, I crane my neck, I turn my eyes that see in opposite directions simultaneous. And I see trees. Are not trees everywhere? And are these forbidden you?

EVE: No, not all trees. Not all fruit. We are given range over all of them, except... *that* tree.

SATAN: Hissss!! And yet it is a tree like any other. What can be God's reason to give you such space and yet blot out that one corner?

EVE: It is a special tree. An exceptional tree. He called it the Tree of Knowledge. Of Good and Evil.

SATAN: Ah, knowledge. Now it is explained. It must be that very knowledge that makes him God. For all other knowledge is known to you, yet you are not God. And *I* am not God! Let us go closer, you and I. Let us explore this tree.

BIRDSONG BECOMES LOUDER

EVE: We are not forbid from looking on it, climbing its branches, picking its leaves to make necklets. No.

SATAN: Oh, I could not climb such a tree. I have such a fear of falling. Only you can climb and reach the fruit.

EVE: I could not eat...

SATAN: (INTERRUPTING): But look. Some of it has fallen already. Windfall, which belongs to all. It lies within my reach. Even one as lowly as I...

LOUD MUNCHING, SLURPING SOUNDS, THEN...

SATAN: Hissss!! Oh, that was good. (BEAT) Delicious, in fact. Sweet. Juicy. A few pips, it's true, but life is full of little pips. And am I hurt by this fruit? And am I changed? Look!

EVE: I cannot see a change. And yet...

SATAN: (VOICE BECOMING INTIMATE): I tell you what I think. I think that God did not mean at all to forbid you this fruit. But seeing your fine and delicate nature, the nature He himself created, and for which he feels overly responsible, He feared you might suffer some digestive upset. A minor medical problem. Irritable bowel syndrome! (BEAT) He is too loving, is God. If He has one fault, which God forbid He should have, then it is: He is too loving. And yet I have shown there is no danger. If you also ate of the fruit and proved Him wrong, I am sure it would be as a weight lifted from His wondrous mind. I am sure He would thank you for such a release. Hisss!!!

EVE: You truly think so?

SATAN: Oh, I do. I do.

EVE: Then I shall eat. I can on tiptoe reach the lowest branch...

SATAN: Do so. Do so.

PAUSE, THEN...

THUNDERCLAP

SATAN: And did it taste well? Hisss!!

EVE: It…it…Aaaaaaaaaaaaaarrrrrrrrrrrggggggggghhh! (SCREAMS)

SATAN: Well, that's it. I'm off. Slither, slither. Always leave them screaming, that's what I say. (LAUGHS, FADES)

FOOTSTEPS RUNNING, GROWING LOUDER

ADAM: Eve! Eve, my wife! What has befallen you?

EVE: My husband! My life! I have… have… I have done…

SHORT SILENCE, THEN EVE MOANS A GREAT MOAN

ADAM: (CALMLY NOW): Oh yes, I see what you have done. You have eaten of the fruit.

EVE: And I have seen…

ADAM: Good and evil…

EVE: Life and death. (BEAT) I have seen death and know not how to speak of it!

ADAM: Then I too shall see death! We must not be separated! Give me! Give me of the fruit!

EVE: No, no! You do not understand. The horror, the horror!

ADAM: Then I will take the fruit! (BEAT) There!

BRIEF SILENCE, THEN ADAM AND EVE BEGIN TO MOAN, THE MOANS GROWING EVER LOUDER, THEN THE ROAR OF LIONS, CHATTER OF MONKEYS, SCREAMS OF BIRDS ARE INTERMINGLED, THEN…

GOD: (SHOUTING): What's happened? What's all this racket? What's all this bloody noise?

ADAM: God has returned! And we are naked!

EVE: This is horrible! You realise what God has done? He's tricked us into taking part in a nude radio programme! It's disgusting! (BEAT) Let us cover ourselves. Let us use the leaves of the Tree of Knowledge.

SOUNDS OF SCRABBLING ABOUT, THEN HEAVY FOOTSTEPS

GOD: Adam, Eve! What's happened? (BEAT) Why, in God's name, are you dressed like a salad?

ADAM: No! Do not look at us!

EVE: We were naked and ashamed!

CRACKLE OF RADIO

SATAN: Listen! Listen, my demons! My work is done. The work of Satan done. Mankind is damned. (LAUGHS)

CRACKLE CEASES

GOD: Who told you that you were naked? (BEAT) No. Don't answer. There's only one answer. He listens as I listen. I know what's in his heart as he knows mine. Satan has done this.

EVE: I am the one to blame. I listened to the voice of evil and I sinned.

GOD: Well, it's something that tha knows it and confesses it. I don't reckon it's much, but it's a start. Every ending is a beginning.

ADAM: We are both to blame.

EVE: Oh no…!

GOD: Oh ay. There's no denying. Thy husband speaks t' truth. And your punishment shall be…

ADAM: We will die.

GOD: Oh yes, but not yet. Not just yet. And in the end… Well, that's another story. (BEAT) For now, and for your disobedience, you've lost the home that sheltered you, the fruits that fed you, the love and trust of the animals surrounding you, the haven that enclosed you with warmth, light and love. You will leave this Paradise. You will be wanderers on the face of the earth, and in due course, in that dark day, yes, yes, you will die. But I do not turn completely from you. You, my first children, shall see my face again and hear my voice. Always you will hear my voice.

ADAM: And will it bring us comfort?

GOD: Not always. Sometimes you and your children will revile me, or find another god, or imagine I was a dream and nothing more. But I am and always will be. (BEAT) A flaming sword will guide you out of Paradise and its flames will prevent your return.

EVE: Is there no hope?

34

GOD: There is always hope. For I will watch over you for ages you cannot calculate, through worlds you cannot imagine.

BRIEF SILENCE

GOD: (HIS VOICE RISES TO A FURIOUS CRESCENDO): Now Go-o-o-o-o-o-o-o!!!!!!!

SOUND OF GREAT RUSHING WIND

MUSIC FADE UP, FADE DOWN

ANNOUNCER: And now for today's episode of At Home with the Nomads, an everyday story of desert folk. Abraham and Sarah travelled to Canaan where Sarah, who is barren, persuaded Abraham to take a second wife. But all is not well... (FADES)

SOAP OPERA MUSIC FADES UP, FADES DOWN, THEN...

ABRAHAM: Abraham's Diary 11th of June, 4,905 BC. (PAUSE) Well, actually I'm not writing my diary today. Time-honoured tradition, habit of a life-time, all ended, gone up in smoke. A whole day missed. And why? Why am I not writing my diary today?

PHARAOH: I am the Pharaoh of Egypt. For many years I have pondered in my deep philosophical manner the misfortunes of the world. (BEAT) Let me suggest why you're not writing your diary today. (BEAT) Is it lack of papyrus owing to the sudden drying-up of the Nile, our sacred river?

ABRAHAM: Not really. I have my own little oasis and the papyrus is quite abundant around my tent, thank you very much, O great and wise king.

PHARAOH: I am the Pharaoh of Egypt. For many years I have studied the problems of my people and devoted myself to their solution. (BEAT) Tell me, Abraham − is it because all your animals have died and you have no more hides on which to scratch the letters of your diary? Is that the reason?

ABRAHAM: Er... no. It's not that either, mighty monarch. My camels continue to thrive, thank you very much, sir.

PHARAOH: Wait! Wait! I, the Pharaoh of Egypt, have the answer! It is because you are chained to the wall in one of my many dungeons and my torturer is about to lash you with his cat of nine tails!

ABRAHAM: Yes! Yes! That's it! (BEAT) Oh, please don't let him do it!

PHARAOH: It is not because of the sudden drying-up of the Nile, but the Nile nonetheless has suddenly and surprisingly dried up. It is not because your animals have died, but it remains the case that everybody else's animals have died, most unexpectedly. I am a great king indeed, but now I suffer a great punishment. My people suffer. Only one man in my kingdom does not suffer these catastrophes. You, Abraham! You do not suffer! Why is that?

ABRAHAM: Maybe I'm just lucky.

PHARAOH: (ANGRY): Lucky? I'll show you lucky!

36

ABRAHAM: (TERRIFIED): No, please! No!

PHARAOH: Why not? Why should you not suffer? Am I not suffering? Do my people not suffer? Tell me, Abraham the nomad!

ABRAHAM: Well, I've suffered too, you know. I can tell you about suffering. All you need to know, Mr Pharaoh. Did I ever tell you about Canaan? God sent us there. And there was a famine. I mean, I don't blame God. He was probably just testing us. But I was very disappointed in Canaan. So I thought: Let's give Egypt a try.

PHARAOH: Now all of Egypt suffers plagues. Boils and carbuncles. Streets full of dead people. The cries of the bereaved.

ABRAHAM: Right. That's not very good, is it?

PHARAOH: Not very good at all, Abraham. So I have to put it to you: Bad luck follows you about.

ABRAHAM: Well, I wouldn't say that.

PHARAOH: Yes, it does. Famine in Canaan, plague in Egypt…

ABRAHAM: Coincidence.

PHARAOH: I don't think so. I think God is angry with me. But I don't know why. (BEAT) I think *you* know, Abraham! Since you're always telling me how close to God you are, I thought I'd pose the question: Why me?

ABRAHAM: Why me? That's a profound question, Mr Pharaoh. For many centuries philosophers and intellectuals have asked themselves that question…

CRACK OF THE WHIP

ABRAHAM: Aaargghhh! No! No! I'm an old man. Can't you see I'm an old man? I can't stand pain. Or even mild discomfort. Please let me go! Unchain me. Tell the man to put away his whip. Please!

PHARAOH: Not till I get some answers. I know it has to do with you. But I don't know what it is. Maybe it's to do with your sister.

ABRAHAM: Sarah? No, I'm sure…

PHARAOH: Yes. I'm certain. But what? (BEAT) Your sister is a beautiful woman. That's why I bought her from you. Maybe I didn't pay enough. Maybe that's why God's angry. Personally, I thought I was quite generous. But God might have different ideas. How much was it now? Let me see. Four oxen, five asses, three manservants and three maidservants, ten camels… Was I not generous enough?

ABRAHAM: No, no. I mean, yes, yes. You were very generous indeed.

PHARAOH: And I have always treated her well. Jewels, clothes, a steam bath in the Greek style with its own jacuzzi, a pair of lion cubs … She's wanted for nothing.

ABRAHAM: It's true, it's true. Don't whip me again!

PHARAOH: All these things taken together. Is this not the going rate for a man's sister? Even in Canaan...

ABRAHAM: Oh yes, By Canaan standards it's more than good. It's top rate.

PHARAOH: Yet God punishes me. Why does he do so?

ABRAHAM: I can't think. I can't imagine. I...

PHARAOH: Because you lied to me! Because Sarah is not your sister! Sarah is your wife!

ABRAHAM: Oh yes. That. But that's just a family thing. A private matter. I didn't think you'd be interested...

PHARAOH: So I have sinned against the Lord by taking another man's wife. And he punishes me and my people. And it's all *your* fault for letting me think she was your sister!

ABRAHAM: I thought you wouldn't like it if you knew. I thought you'd have me killed.

PHARAOH: Well, now I'm going to get rid of you...

ABRAHAM: Oh no! Please...

PHARAOH: Take your wife and your tents and your family, and go! Leave my country forever!

ABRAHAM: Can I also take the four oxen, five asses, three manservants, three maidservants, and ten camels?

PHARAOH: No!

ABRAHAM: Is that final?

CRACK OF WHIP

ABRAHAM: Aaargghhh!! (PAUSE) Alright then. I accept your offer.

SOAP OPERA MUSIC FADE UP, FADE DOWN

ANNOUNCER: Will Abraham's luck take a turn for the better? Tune in tomorrow.

CRIME THRILLER MUSIC FADE UP, FADE DOWN. THEN...

GOD: Hello again, radio fans. God here. Yes, I'm back. (BEAT) Now. Murder. There. That's got you interested. When I look at the evil that men do, I'm surprised. Ay. And also I'm *not* surprised. Both together. (BEAT) Now. I've had some letters recently about Cain and Abel. It's all to do with my being on the wireless. People like to write in with their questions. And some people wanted to know if I thought Cain was really guilty. I think there's some society been founded called *Cain is Innocent OK* by people who think he was the victim of a government conspiracy. After all, folk love a good murder mystery. So I thought we'd do a reconstruction. The people you are about to hear are, of course, merely actors.

FADE DOWN, FADE UP

ABEL: Hello there. Hello Cain, my brother.

CAIN: Good morning, Abel. How are the sheep today?

ABEL: Oh, a little bit frisky. One of them ran away on Friday. But I went after it…

CAIN: Oh yes, I knew you'd go after it. You're that sort of shepherd. Conscientious. Everybody knows how conscientious you are.

ABEL: Well, it's nice of you to say so, Cain.

CAIN: Oh, everybody notices. Dad notices. Mum notices…

ABEL: Well, yes. They're bound to. There's not many of us people about yet. They're bound to notice things, our mum and dad, Adam and Eve…

CAIN: And God. God notices.

ABEL: Oh right. God. Yes, God is bound to notice…

CAIN: God was very pleased with that ram you sacrificed last Sunday. I could tell.

ABEL: He's probably just being polite. I've always found him very polite.

CAIN: No, no. I think he was genuine. That's one thing I've noticed about God. He's always genuine.

ABEL: The one true God.

CAIN: Quite. (BEAT) He wasn't so pleased about my offering.

ABEL: Oh, I'm sure he was.

CAIN: No, no. I cannot tell a lie. I don't think he was very pleased at all.

ABEL: Well, it's vegetables, isn't it? You grow crops...

CAIN: Crops are important.

ABEL: Yes, they are. I didn't say they weren't. I'm sure God thinks so too. But they're not very dramatic.

CAIN: Some people think you just have to throw the seeds on the ground and they grow by themselves.

ABEL: Oh no, I'm sure God doesn't think that.

CAIN: What people don't realise is the amount of work involved.

ABEL: I know you like to be organic. None of that chemical rubbish.

CAIN: And the heartache.

ABEL: Heartache?

CAIN: You plant the buggers and you pray for rain. Or sometimes you pray for sunshine. And sometimes it doesn't happen.

ABEL: But I think the weather's been pretty good lately. That's something you can thank God for. He's given you just the right weather all year round...

CAIN: People don't understand you can't always win prizes. Even with good weather. Sometimes the spinach isn't

42

green enough or the corn isn't yellow enough. And it's not your fault.

ABEL: Have you ever considered maybe crops are not your big talent? Maybe you could do something else.

CAIN: What else is there?

ABEL: We might get some cattle. We've got plenty of grazing land…

CAIN: No, no, it would take up too much of my time.

ABEL: But if you're not cut out for crops…

CAIN: What I've always thought is: I might be a natural hunter/gatherer. Then my time would be my own. I could wander about…

ABEL: Hunting and gathering…

CAIN: Nobody judging me. Nobody interfering…

ABEL: I don't know so much about hunter/gathering. I don't know that it's really the career for you. It needs a lot of patience…

CAIN: I've *got* patience.

ABEL: I mean my sheep need all the patience I can give them. God only knows. But hunter/gathering. Oh dear. I don't think I could do that. It means lying in wait for things. Antelope. Elephant. Whatever. Waiting very patiently till they come by to drink at the waterhole…

43

CAIN: *I* could do that.

ABEL: And when they don't come by, there's lots of hard work in gathering too. All those berries.

CAIN: *I* can pick berries.

ABEL: But knowing which are good to eat and which are poisonous…

CAIN: I can *learn*.

ABEL: All those different colours. And shapes. And I've not even got on to mushrooms yet.

CAIN: I *like* mushrooms.

ABEL: But some of them won't like *you*. Some of those mushrooms are deadly. Oh I know it wasn't always so. When our mum and dad were young and the lion lay down with the lamb, all those vegetables were friendly too. But times have changed.

CAIN: *I* could do it. I could be a good hunter/gatherer. Look, I've got the knife.

ABEL: Oh yes, that's a good knife. I can see. Very sharp blade. Good for hunting and gathering both. Cut the deer's throat, pull up a mushroom. I can see you've been thinking about this. But the patience thing…

CAIN: *I* can be patient. When I feel like it.

ABEL: But you do have a bit of a temper. You are sometimes a bit contrary…

44

CAIN: No, I'm not.

ABEL: Well, gosh, dear brother, I certainly don't want to be the one to contradict you. But you *do* have quite a temper. You were quite short with the angel Uriel the other day. And all he did was walk about a bit.

CAIN: He can't just walk where he pleases. I'd just planted cabbages.

ABEL: Even so…

CAIN: Who do these angels think they are anyway, just walking about wherever it pleases them? It's not as if they can't fly.

ABEL: Well, probably their wings get tired…

CAIN: You're always making excuses for them. And always making excuses for God. It doesn't matter to you that he's constantly rejecting my salads. You're his favourite, that's what it is. I know your little game. Sucking up all the time. (SINGS) Abel, Abel, puts meat on the table! (BACK TO SPEAKING VOICE) And it's not fair! It's just not fair!

ABEL: Have a bit of a care, brother. Don't forget the knife. (PANIC) The knife! The knife!

HORRENDOUS SCREAM. IT FADES, THEN…

CAIN: Oh God, what have I done? I've killed Abel! (BEAT) Well, he deserved it anyway. Always baiting me. Always teasing me about how his sheep have got every right to eat my grass. (BEAT) Oh God, oh God! (BEAT) No, I don't think I'd better call on God. Not this time. I know. I'll hide the body. Nobody will miss him.

SOUNDS OF BODY BEING DRAGGED AWAY, THEN FADE...

FADE UP BIRDSONG. THEN...

GOD: A new day dawns! O beauteous day! Now I wonder what's happened to Abel, my shepherd? (SHOUTS) Cain, Cain! Where's young Abel this morning?

Cain: (WHISPERED ASIDE): It's God. I knew he'd come snooping around. But I can fool him. I'll just act daft. (SHOUTS) Hello, God! Good morning to you! Very nice day! Thanks for all the good weather lately! And thanks for coming round so often! It's always good to see you! (WHISPERED ASIDE) I think I've got away with it. I don't think he suspects.

VOICE FADES. FADE UP OWL HOOTS, THEN...

KNOCKING ON DOOR.

MICHAEL: (SHOUTING): Hello in there! Anybody home?

SOUND OF DOOR OPENING

EVE: Who's there? It's dark and I can't see.

MICHAEL: It's Inspector Michael...

GABRIEL: And Sergeant Gabriel...

MICHAEL: The Flying Squad. (LAUGHS) Good evening to you, Eve, mother of Mankind... (BEAT) And is your husband, Adam, father of Mankind, at home tonight?

EVE: Of course he is. Where'd you expect him to be? It's not as if there's places to go and people to see.

MICHAEL: May we come in? (BEAT) I can always get a search warrant.

EVE: Oh no, don't be like that, Mr Michael sir, come on in.

ADAM: (SHOUTS): Who is it, Eve, old girl?

EVE: It's Michael and Gabriel. Who were you expecting, Adam? (BEAT) Have a couple of seats, officers.

MICHAEL: If it's all the same to you, we'll just flap our wings and hover.

EVE: As you please.

SOUND OF FOOTSTEPS

ADAM: Ah, hello there. Welcome, officers. Now, what's it all about, Mr Michael?

MICHAEL: We've had a missing persons report...

ADAM: I'll ask the wife if we've seen any missing persons lately. (CLEARS HIS THROAT) Eve, my love! Have we seen any missing persons lately?

EVE: What do these missing persons look like?

MICHAEL: What do these missing persons look like, sergeant?

GABRIEL: I'll consult my notes, sir. (COUGHS, READS) Young man, sunburnt as befits an outdoor type; normally wearing garments of wool as befits a shepherd; medium height as befits the younger brother of another young man of medium height and son of father also of medium height.

ADAM (THE PENNY DROPS): Hang on, they're talking about our Abel!

EVE: Oh God, what's happened to him?

MICHAEL: God doesn't know. That's why he called us.

ADAM: I don't believe God doesn't know.

MICHAEL: Have you seen your younger son recently, Mr Adam?

ADAM: No, no. But I've seen quite a bit of Cain today. Fair blocked out the sun, he did.

MICHAEL: Cain? Sergeant, do we have any previous on a person called Cain?

GABRIEL: Let me look at my notes, sir. Ah yes. Cain. (BEAT) Vegetable and crop grower. Dirty complexion as befits man working with soil all day. Habitually wears ill-fitting cotton smock as befits crop grower with little talent for weaving.

MICHAEL: And is this Cain person here, Mr Adam? Mrs Eve?

EVE: He's in his room. Practising knife-throwing. He's getting quite good. (SHOUTS) Cain! Cain! Come on out! It's the police!

SILENCE, THEN HURRIED FOOTSTEPS...

CAIN: What do you lot want with *me* then? Haven't you got anything better to do?

MICHAEL: No, actually. It's one of the problems of Eternity – lethargy creeps in. (BEAT) I have to ask you, Mr Cain, did you murder your brother Mr Abel?

CAIN: No.

MICHAEL: Really?

CAIN: Well, it wasn't my fault. It was an accident. He ran on to the knife.

MICHAEL: Sorry, Mr Cain, that's not good enough. We've heard it all before.

GABRIEL: No we haven't, sir. This is our first murder case.

MICHAEL (ANNOYED): Thank you sergeant. (BEAT) Mr Cain, I am charging you with the murder of your brother Mr Abel, professional shepherd of Gambol Meadows, East of Eden. And I must warn you that anything you say will be taken down and may be used in a book that will last several thousand years and be translated into many languages...

CAIN: Alright. I'll go quiet. It's a fair cop, guv.

EVE: (DISTRAUGHT): What's going to happen to him?

MICHAEL: Well, there's no actual precedent, but I imagine he'll be banished to the Land of Nod and marked about the face to make sure he is easily identifiable to any future inhabitants who may happen on the same location.

ADAM: I can't believe it. We've never had a murderer in our family before.

MICHAEL: Perhaps, Mr Adam, you should console yourself with the thought that you've also never had a plumber, carpenter, builder, circus clown, public relations consultant, haberdasher or indeed librarian. (BEAT) Come with us, Mr Cain. It's time to go.

CRIME THRILLER MUSIC, THEN...

GOD: Right. God here. So you see, listeners, the right man *was* convicted, even though he had no previous. Truth to tell, there weren't a whole lot of suspects in them days.

MUSIC FADE UP, FADE DOWN

ANNOUNCER: And now for today's episode of At Home with the Nomads, an everyday story of desert folk. Abraham, Sarah and Hagar have left Egypt but their problems continue. The two women have fallen out...

SOAP OPERA MUSIC FADE UP, FADE DOWN...

ABRAHAM: Abraham's Diary 9th of July, 4,900 BC. (PAUSE) When will my troubles ever end? Do I get any respect? Not from these women. They don't know the meaning of the word. You'd think God would fix it so I

50

don't have any day-to-day worries, so I can just get on with the big job… (VOICE FADES)

HAGAR: Sarah, I don't know why we don't get on any more. We used to be friends. And we have a lot in common.

SARAH: Hagar, we *don't* have a lot in common. We have only *one* thing in common and that's Abraham! How do you think I feel about that? How can you expect me to be friends with you when you've just given birth to my husband's son?

HAGAR: But it was you who suggested it!

SARAH: How can we be friends when you used to be a servant girl and now you're my equal?

HAGAR: But it was you told Abraham to marry me. (BEAT) Anyway, I always do the washing up. And I still take out the slops.

SARAH: How can we be friends when you have a lovely baby and I have nothing?

HAGAR: Ah. Yes. He's lovely, my Ishmael. My pride and joy.

SARAH BEGINS TO CRY

HAGAR: Don't cry, Sarah. It's not too late for you!

SARAH: Yes it is. It's always been too late for me!

HAGAR: Hush now, hush. Here comes Abraham. Pull yourself together. Don't let him see you like this.

SARAH: (SNIFFLING): I'll try!

ABRAHAM: Oh, life is wonderful! Yes, it is. Snatch the day, that's what I say!

HAGAR: Something must have happened, Abraham. Something to make you cheerful.

ABRAHAM: I've just seen God.

HAGAR: Ask him in. We can give him a cup of wine.

ABRAHAM: No, no. He had to go. Couldn't stay long at all. Just wanted a brief word with me. (BEAT) God has given me a vision. (BEAT) First he told me to count the stars in the heavens. So I did.

HAGAR: How many are there?

ABRAHAM: I'm not sure. I actually didn't get very far...

SARAH: Once you ran out of fingers...

HAGAR: Wasn't God annoyed that you didn't pay attention?

ABRAHAM: Don't be silly, Hagar! I mean, it was just a ploy. Just to get me looking beyond the every-day world. And then God said to me: *Your offspring will be as numerous as the stars.*

SARAH: (SARCASTICALLY): Oh, this really makes me happy, Abraham! This really raises my spirits!

ABRAHAM: So it should, Sarah. For God has prophesied that you too shall have a child. And we shall call him Isaac.

SARAH: Don't be silly.

ABRAHAM: No, it's true. God told me.

SARAH: (LAUGHING) That's ridiculous.

ABRAHAM: Now, now. If God says it, it can't be ridiculous. If God says it, he won't like the fact that you're laughing at him.

Sarah (SUDDENLY NERVOUS): Laugh at God? Me? No, no. It's a frog in my throat. A bit of a cough. The nights are getting cold again.

HAGAR: Abraham, what's that knife for?

ABRAHAM: What knife, Hagar?

HAGAR: The knife in your hand.

ABRAHAM: Which hand?

HAGAR: The one you're hiding behind your back.

ABRAHAM: Ah yes. This one. (BEAT) Well, God and I made a covenant. He promised my children the world…

HAGAR: And what did you have to promise *Him*?

ABRAHAM: Let me explain (BEAT) about circumcision…

SOAP OPERA MUSIC FADE UP, FADE DOWN

53

ANNOUNCER: Will Abraham's new religious ritual prove popular? Will Sarah and Hagar grow fonder of each other once they are both mothers? Tune in tomorrow.

CRACKLE OF RADIO, THEN EPIC MOVIE MUSIC FADES UP, FADES DOWN

NOAH: (SHOUTS): Oh God, your servant Noah calls out to you! Oh, that I am come to such a place! Oh God, that we are come to such a world as this, where men have deserted you and your word, and laugh to scorn your creation and your teachings!

HAM: Noah, my father, if you love God and love not this hot and unclean part of earth, in heaven's name why did you come here?

NOAH: Ham, my son, I came here for the waters.

HAM: The waters? What waters? We're in the middle of the desert.

NOAH: I was misinformed. (PAUSE) Oh the heat-hazed, blasted desert, the orange sun that battles with my screwed-up eyes! But now I'm here, I'm going to make a go of it. I'm not going to have people say that Noah wasn't a goer!

HAM: Dad, I admire that. I suppose you're going to irrigate the land and put an awning on the front of our tent to protect us from the sun.

NOAH: I might. (PAUSE) Or I might (BEAT) build an ark!

HAM: Build an ark? What's an ark?

54

NOAH: I don't know. Yes, I do. At least I think I do. It's a big boat! (WHISPERED ASIDE) Now why did I say that? It makes no sense. My mind must be wandering.

HAM: It's the sun. It's addled your brain. Maybe you should get that awning put up right away.

NOAH: Yes, you're right. Boat? Boat? What am I thinking about? I'm getting old.

HAM: I'll go off and dig some ditches then, if that's Ok. Can't have irrigation without ditches. (BEAT) Dad, are you going to be allright if I leave you on your own?

NOAH: Of course I will.

HAM: You won't go building any big boats while I'm gone, will you?

NOAH: Big boats? Preposterous! (LAUGHS) No. Don't worry, Ham. It was just a slip of the tongue.

HAM: And you won't go talking to any strange people while I'm gone? You know what you're like these days. Bad tempered. Drinking too much. Always picking fights. (BEAT) Dad, what's in that leather carrier?

NOAH: What leather carrier? (BEAT) Oh, you mean *this* leather carrier?

HAM: The one with the cork in the top. That's the one I mean.

NOAH: Don't you worry, Ham my son. It's only water. Pure, unadulterated one hundred per cent proof water. From the

55

mountain stream. Your brother Shem brought it down for me.

HAM: My brother Shem is too soft on you. Too easily swayed. Well, if you're going to drink, see you don't have too much.

NOAH: I'll just stay here and meditate. Think about God. If anybody talks to me, I'll just not answer.

HAM: Good. See you don't. See you later, Dad.

FOOTSTEPS FADE AWAY

NOAH: Goodbye, my son. (VOICE DROPS) Don't you worry. No, no. I'm fine. Big boats, hah! (BEAT) Now. It would be nice to find a bit of shade. Yes indeed.

THUNDERCLAP

NOAH: Aaagghhh!! A darkness falls upon me! I'm blind! I'm blind!

GOD: No, tha's not, Noah. Tha's not blind.

NOAH: What do you mean I'm not blind? I should know whether I'm blind or not. It's *my* eyes we're talking about. I'll show you blind, I will! I'd show you blind if I could only see you to begin with!

GOD: Moan, moan, moan. (BEAT) I'm God, of course, so I get it all the time. But somehow I never get bloody used to it. (BEAT) Now, when I tell thee tha's not blind, Noah, then tha can take it from me tha's not blind. Because I'm

God and I know. You asked for shade so I let thee walk in my shadow. That's all. Your eyes will get used to it.

NOAH: I hope you're right about that. You shouldn't creep up on people, you and your shadow. (BEAT) Oh, forgive me, Lord. I know I'm just a grumpy old man. But it's *your* fault really. You've let this world go to rack and ruin.

GOD: Well, the buck stops here. But I've got a plan. (BEAT) Noah, tha may be a sinful man who drinks too much but tha's still the best man I know. Which shows thee how bad things are. So. Appen I'm going to save thee.

NOAH: Save me from what?

GOD: From the catastrophe that's about to overwhelm thee. From the great flood.

NOAH: (LAUGHS): Flood? Here?

GOD: That's right. The one thing that's going to save thee is…

NOAH: (THE PENNY DROPS): …build a boat.

GOD: Yes. Build a boat. Tha's pretty quick on the uptake today.

NOAH: (HORROR STRUCK): Oh no!

GOD: And just to show I'm a fair God, honest and open, blunt and down-to-earth, completely transparent in my dealings with Mankind, thee can tell all thy neighbours and get them to tell all *their* neighbours. A bit like Twitter.

NOAH: Tell them there's a flood coming? What will they do?

GOD: Nothing. But then it's their decision.

NOAH: Let me get this straight, God. You want me to tell them there's a great flood coming?

GOD: Yes.

NOAH: In the middle of the desert?

GOD: That's right. Tell them it's an act of God.

NOAH: They won't believe it. They think I'm a fool. They think I drink too much.

GOD: And they're right. Thee is a fool. And tha does drink too much.

NOAH: They'll laugh at me.

GOD: They laugh at thee already. What has tha got to lose?

NOAH: My sons will laugh at me.

GOD: You're their father. They may think tha's mad, but they'll do as tha says. They'll help thee...

NOAH: ...build a boat?

GOD: Yes. That's what sons do. They obey their father. Even when they shouldn't. Take that Shem for instance. He shouldn't be bringing thee wine every day. But he does. Sons are naturally obedient. (BEAT) Now. I happen to be carrying the plans.

NOAH: What plans?

GOD: The plans for the boat. Here. Take a look at these. I'll spread them out on the sand. Get me a couple of rocks, will you? To hold it down. There. (BEAT) As tha can see, it will be made of gopher wood, smeared inside and out with pitch, with three decks and lots of internal compartments. It will be 300 cubits long, 50 cubits wide, and 30 cubits high; it will have a roof finished to a cubit upward, and an entrance on the side. Now, isn't that impressive? I call it The Ark.

NOAH: Why?

GOD: Because, lad, I'm God and I call it what I like.

NOAH: It's very big. (BEAT) I've only got three wives and four sons and a few daughters-in-law that I haven't counted lately. That's a very big boat for us.

GOD: Ah, but you won't be alone. You'll be taking all the animals.

NOAH: All the animals?

GOD: Well, not every single individual dog and parrot and aardvark. But every animal in the sense of two of every kind, a male and a female. To keep the species going.

NOAH: That's a lot of animals.

GOD: It's a big boat. As you said.

NOAH: It'll take a long time to build. And what about the heat and the dust … What about all those health and safety issues? My sons won't like it. The National Union of Boat Builders and Maritime Crafts won't like it.

GOD: The biggest health and safety issue as far as you lot are concerned is what will happen if you don't get it built on time. Tell *that* to the Union. Unless they're very good swimmers.

NOAH: Look, God, I've always been your most loyal follower. I've defended you when people said you weren't up to the job. Now you're going to throw it all over…

GOD: Make a new beginning.

NOAH: And you pick me, an old drunk, to be your messenger.

GOD: I do.

NOAH: Why?

GOD: I'm an equal opportunity employer. (BEAT) Well, I've said all I'm going to say.

NOAH: But I've not even started…

GOD: Don't talk to *me*. Talk to your sons. Goodbye! (VOICE FADES)

EPIC MOVIE MUSIC FADES UP, FADES DOWN

NOAH: And we're going to build this boat.

GENERAL UPROAR FADING TO BACKGROUND HUBBUB OF VOICES

NEIGHBOUR: (SHOUTING ABOVE THE HUBBUB): Look, Mr Noah, we've been neighbours a good many years now…

NOAH: True, Mr Neighbour. Very true.

NEIGHBOUR: And I've put up with a lot! (BEAT) But if you're planning to build this huge boat in your front yard… which is right next door to me…

NOAH: Which I *am*. God help me. And it *is*, God help us both.

NEIGHBOUR: …you'll be blocking our view. (BEAT) Look. I did twenty years as a goat-slaughterer. I saved my shekels. Now the wife and me, we've got a nice little camper model with a good view of the sands. And you come along and say you're going to build a giant boat right in front of our window, blocking our access. And that's just the start. All these animals you've been talking about. The noise! The smell! The danger! All those lions, tigers, elephants, rats… (BEAT) I presume you'll be taking rats?

NOAH: I'm afraid so.

NEIGHBOUR:Now, I'm a great animal lover myself. As much as you can be when you're a goat slaughterer. But you have to draw the line somewhere. (BEAT) I ask you, Mr Noah – this whole boat thing – is it fair?

NOAH: I didn't say it was fair. Fair is a word I don't often use. But it's God's will.

NEIGHBOUR: Because we're going to have this great flood of yours!

61

GENERAL LAUGHTER FADES UP, FADES DOWN, THEN...

NEIGHBOUR: Well, Mr Noah, I say you can't do it without planning permission. And I'm getting up a petition right now to make my views known to the council. (BEAT) So the next thing you can expect is a visit from the planning inspector. There! Good day to you, Mr Noah.

NOAH: Good day to you, Mr Neighbour.

GENERAL SOUNDS OF CHAIR SCRAPING, FOOTSTEPS, MOANING VOICES, PEOPLE SHOUTING GOODBYE

NOAH: Goodbye to all of you, neighbours!

CROWD SOUND FADES

HAM: Well, dad, that didn't last long. Shortest neighbourhood meeting we've had in a long time. They didn't even stay to finish the wine.

NOAH: Ham, my son, I know you think I've lost my mind this time. Sometimes I think so too. But we've got to do God's will.

HAM: OK, I've been talking it over with Shem and Japheth. We'll humour you. For now. But this whole thing is mad. The big test is going to be this animal thing. If you think all the animals in the world...

NOAH: No, no, only two of each.

HAM: ... are going to walk into our front yard and offer themselves for a boat trip in the desert, you're sadly mistaken.

SUDDEN ROAR OF LIONS, TRUMPET OF ELEPHANTS, LAUGH OF HYENAS, THEN...

NOAH: It's started. My God, look out there! It's started already.

SCREECH OF EAGLES, BARKING OF DOGS, MOOING OF COWS, THEN...

HAM: Show us those plans again, Dad. I think we'd better make a start. (VOICE FADES)

SERIOUS RADIO MUSIC FADES UP, FADES DOWN, THEN...

ANNOUNCER: And now for something completely different. Something far more serious and intensely relevant to modern life. This week's edition of the popular Jacob Israel phone-in programme is focusing on the problems of twins. Take it away, Jacob...

SERIOUS RADIO MUSIC FADES UP, FADES DOWN,

THEN...

JACOB: Many thanks for that introduction. Yes, it's Jacob Israel looking at the real issues of modern life. And yes, today we're looking at the problems of twins. It's a fascinating subject and we're waiting for your phone calls. You all know the number: Two-two-two-two. (BEAT) As I'm sure many of you know, I'm particularly interested in the problems of twins because I'm a twin. And being a twin does create lots of difficult situations. I know from first-hand experience. So I want you to share your experiences with me and all my other listeners – including of course all the other twins out there.

RINGING TONE

JACOB: We've got somebody on the line already. (BEAT) Hello, caller. Can I have your name, please?

ESAU: It's Esau.

JACOB: Esau. Oh my God!

ESAU: Yes, Jacob. This is Esau. Thought you could fool me, eh? Changing your name. Jacob Israel indeed! Why can't you stick with your real name? Why can't you just be Jacob Isaacson?

JACOB (EMBARRASSED): I must explain to listeners that this is indeed my own twin brother Esau. And we've not actually spoken for a number of years. Well, Esau, how's it going with you?

ESAU: How's it going with *me*? A lot better than you thought it would be going. Oh, you can call yourself Israel or whatever name you want, but I knew it was you as soon as I heard your voice. You're always so smarmy. That's what gives you away. Did you think you'd get away from me if you went all anonymous?

JACOB: Look, Esau, it's a thing with people in showbiz. Sometime we change our names. It doesn't mean anything. (BEAT) Well, listeners, this is certainly an emotional

64

moment. My long-lost brother has come back to me. (LAUGHS)

ESAU: Not *quite* come back to you. Not quite. Not to the point where I could actually lay hands on you!

JACOB: Lay hands on me! (LAUGHS) I have to explain to the listeners at this point that Esau is a very physical guy, always has been, always doing hunting and stuff, quite violent things I don't really approve of if I'm honest. And I guess if he were here in this studio with me, we'd be hugging each other like mad. Just the way we did when we were kids. Anyway, I'm really glad you got in touch, Esau.

ESAU: Are you? That's nice. (BEAT) It's true I'm the outdoor type, Jacob. It's true I'm very strong and physical. And hairy. Unlike you. Unlike you, my smooth-skinned girly brother. Right now, I'd like to get my fingers round your throat and show your bloody neck how physical I can be.

JACOB (LAUGHS MORE DESPERATELY): Typical Esau. Always clowning around. Him kidding *me*. Me kidding *him*. Us kidding each other. (FINALLY LOSES HIS COOL) Violence solves everything for you, doesn't it? You've always been a bully, never giving me a chance.

ESAU: Me? A bully? Rubbish! When we were born, Jacob, I was born first. Not by much. But enough. Don't you forget that. And even then you were hanging on to my ankle, trying to get ahead of me even before I was born.

JACOB: I can't help it if I'm competitive, Esau. That's modern life. Get used to it.

ESAU: And you always made jokes about my red hair. Yes you did, Jacob! *Ginger!* I got so sick of being called Ginger!

JACOB: Grow up, Esau! If that's the worst thing that ever happens to you, you'll be a lucky man! (CATCHING HIMSELF) Not that I approve of personal insults, of course, especially those that could be construed as racist. But when you're very young...

ESAU: And then you had to steal my birthright. Tell that to your precious listeners! If *you* don't, I will! I'm going to tell them how mean you were! I came home tired and hungry from the hunt. And all I did was ask for a bowl of stew. And you said: "Give me your birthright and I'll give you a bowl of stew." So I said OK. I was only joking. I never thought you were serious.

JACOB: Well, I'd been cooking all day. And it wasn't as if you'd actually caught anything except a very small rabbit. Personally, I was afraid of myxemetosis. Call that a day's hunting? I don't call *that* a day's hunting!

ESAU: And if that wasn't bad enough, you went to our poor father Isaac, who was dying and was practically blind.

JACOB: Listeners, I have to tell you here that he was no more than a little bit poorly and a trifle short-sighted...

ESAU: And you pretended to be me. And you got some goatskin and put it over your arms so you could pretend to be hairy, like me. And he gave you his blessing, my birthright, because he thought you were me.

66

JACOB: No, no, you've got it wrong. I only put the goatskin on because I was cold. So don't make such a thing of it! I'm sure the listeners won't believe all this nonsense for a minute. Anyway, I'll tell them all what happened next. You swore to kill me.

ESAU: Yes, I did. And if I'd done it, no jury would have convicted me. It's a good job I can't get at you now. You always have to hide behind things, don't you? You always have to run away.

JACOB: That's not fair. I suppose you're going on about my trip to Hanan. But the truth is I went there to get married. I was in love with Rachel and I went to her father and asked for her hand. And he said I could have her if I worked seven years for him. So I did. I had a hard life. Being a shepherd isn't easy, you know.

ESAU: Huh!

JACOB: And then he tricked me. (BEAT) I hope you listeners are listening properly here because it shows what a hard life I've had. *Really* hard. But I don't go on about it all the time like my brother. I don't blame other people for the things that happen to me! (BEAT) When the wedding was over and the bride took her veil off, it wasn't Rachel at all. It turned out to be Leah, her older sister. And you know what her father said?

ESAU: Go on then. You're dying to tell me. Go ahead!

JACOB: I'm *not* telling you! I wouldn't be bothered to tell you anything! I'm telling my listeners. (BEAT) He said the older sister always had to marry first. He said he was surprised I didn't know that.

ESAU: Serves you right! At last you got what was coming to you!

JACOB: Seven more years I had to work to get the girl I loved! But I did it. I've worked hard for everything I've got. You talk about me as if I had an easy life, but I didn't. (BEAT) And I've had trouble with my children. Maybe you didn't know about that!

ESAU: Yes I did. I know you had sons. The kind of sons you deserve! I heard they got together and sold your youngest son into slavery!

JACOB: No, no, that's completely untrue. It's Joseph you're taking about. And I can assure you that the slavery story is nonsense. It wasn't slavery at all. It was a very good job opportunity in the Egyptian civil service and he had to leave in a hurry to get to the interview. No, no, I'm not having the slavery bit. It's a well-known fact that Joseph did alright for himself. In the end.

ESAU: All I know is that you're a terrible brother. But what really annoys me is: God likes you. He actually *likes* you.

JACOB: Loves me. God *loves* me actually. But he loves you too, Esau. And I want to say to all my listeners out there that he also loves you listeners, every one.

ESAU: And you think that makes everything OK?

JACOB: Well. Bearable. I think it makes everything bearable. Even our Joseph in the Egyptian civil service. (BEAT) Look, Esau, now we're talking again…

ESAU: Yes?

JACOB: Do you fancy a drink? When I'm through for the day? There's a pub round the corner from here…

ESAU: (UNSURE): Well. (BEAT) OK. What time?

JACOB: Good. See you about five o'clock then.

ESAU: OK. See you.

PHONE GOES DEAD, THEN SHORT SILENCE, THEN PHONE RINGS

JACOB: Hello, caller. What's your name then…. ? (VOICE FADES)

CRACKLE OF RADIO

ANNOUNCER: And now for today's episode of At Home with the Nomads, an everyday story of desert folk. Abraham is feeling pretty good for once, but we all know what God's like – he's always got a card up his sleeve.

SOAP OPERA MUSIC FADE UP, FADE DOWN

ABRAHAM: O God, this is Abraham here. You hear us when we call. I think of our father Adam and mother Eve who devoured the apple of knowledge and were banished from Paradise. I think of their sons, Cain who slew Abel, of the wars and murders that have since become our daily lot. I myself have two great sons, though I don't see much of Ishmael any more. He's gone off to seek his fortune. Still, Isaac remains – and he is the apple of my eye.

GOD: Abraham, Abraham, good to hear thy voice again!

ABRAHAM: And I hear *your* voice, O God! But I don't see you! Is this really God who calls me?

GOD: You don't see me but I see you. (BEAT) Isn't this the time of day you usually write your diary?

ABRAHAM: Oh, I've given up on diaries. I think it's because I'm more confident these days. I read a scroll called *Nomad is an Island*. It's a sort of health manual for travelling folk. And it told me that keeping a diary was very unhealthy. Keeping tabs on yourself all the time. Not good at all.

GOD: I'm sorry about that. I used to enjoy reading what tha thought about things.

ABRAHAM: (SURPRISED): Did you really?

GOD: No, not really. I knew thy every thought anyway. I was just being polite. Because I like thee.

ABRAHAM: I know you like me, but I don't know why. I'm not at all brave, for a start. In fact, I'm a coward.

GOD: No, tha's not brave at all. But I sort of like people with faults. Anyway, I still love Mankind, still put him first, though my ways are not transparent to you. If thee is true to me I'll see thee allright.

ABRAHAM: Have I not travelled far and sought you? Have I ever given up the quest you put on me? How can you doubt my love and loyalty?

GOD: Ah. I have a new task for thee.

ABRAHAM: Another task? Yet another? (BEAT) Small or large?

GOD: Small for me, large for thee.

ABRAHAM: As usual. (BEAT) What is this task?

GOD: Each day tha sacrifices to me – a lamb, an ox, the birds of the air. But know now I do not care for burnt offerings, nor the blood of animals.

ABRAHAM: You've always been compassionate. Tell me how to do your pleasure, win your favour, and I shall fulfil your wish.

GOD: Oh Abraham, take care what tha says. Take care what thee intends.

ABRAHAM: I intend to serve you, Lord; I intend to do Your will where my first parents failed. I repent their rebellion and wish to make amends.

GOD: You, Abraham, have warmed my heart. I look upon thee with my mercy and with love.

ABRAHAM: (JOYOUSLY): It is no more than Your due, You who have created all!

71

GOD: Then I shall tell thee of the sacrifice I demand. I shall tell thee of the sacrifice tha so willingly gives. I demand the life of thy son Isaac. The life of Isaac, thy son.

ABRAHAM: (HORRIFIED): No, Lord, no! No father can sacrifice his son! You cannot ask it! It is beyond...

GOD: Belief? *Is* it beyond belief? Is it beyond thy belief in me?

SILENCE, THEN...

GOD: Will thee then do this for me? Or have thee taken on thyself the ways of thy first parents? Is the strain of disobedience indestructible?

SILENCE, LABOURED BREATHING OF ABRAHAM, THEN...

ABRAHAM: Lord God, is this truly Your will?

GOD: Truly. As true as thee is true. As true as thee has promised to be true.

SILENCE, THEN...

GOD: Well? Well, my Abraham?

ABRAHAM: What You say is well, for You are God. But...

GOD: Well?

ABRAHAM: It is well. I will do it. I will do as You demand. I will do it well.

GOD: And well shall come of well. As evil has come from evil.

ABRAHAM: So we must believe. But...

GOD: But?

ABRAHAM: But why... ?

GOD: But me no buts. I am God.

ABRAHAM: (WITH RESIGNATION) But then it shall be done.

GOD: And shall be done well. I am well pleased. I leave thee now. (VOICE OF GOD FADES)

PAUSE

ABRAHAM: (SHOUTS): Isaac, come to me! Hear me!

RUNNING FOOTSTEPS

ISAAC: I come, father. I am ready. What is your bidding?

ABRAHAM: My son, my son, do you love me as you say?

ISAAC: You are my father. I love you. As you love God, our Father in heaven.

ABRAHAM: And do you obey me? Will you carry out whatever I instruct?

ISAAC: Why, do I not always? And always I shall. As you obey your Father in heaven.

ABRAHAM: (WRACKED WITH EMOTION): Oh God, Oh God...!

ISAAC: You call on Him. And when you call on Him, He speaks with you.

ABRAHAM: And He has spoken. Already He has spoken today. (BEAT) Look, it is the time of sacrifice. We must go, you and I, to the hilltop, to the stone altar of the Lord. There we will make sacrifice.

ISAAC: Small duty indeed. For we love God for His goodness. Let us go.

ABRAHAM: Bring the knife that we use at such times.

ISAAC: The very one.

ABRAHAM: And bring the rope that shall bind the offering.

ISAAC: So I do. (VOICE FADES)

WIND BLOWING, FADE UP, FADE DOWN. THEN...

ABRAHAM: Now we are at the place of sacrifice, let us perform this business. You have the knife, Isaac?

ISAAC: As I spoke, so I have done, my father. Here it is. (BEAT) And yet we have brought no object for the sacrifice. No ox or lamb or fowl. (BEAT) Well, we must trust in God to provide the beast.

ABRAHAM: Yes. He will provide the beast. Of that I have no doubt.

ISAAC: And how long shall we wait?

ABRAHAM: We wait as God bids, no more no less. Though I do not think our wait is long.

ISAAC: Do you then see the beast we must sacrifice? I scan the hilltop but I see nothing.

ABRAHAM: And yet I see all. I see the sacrifice.

ISAAC (LAUGHS): Oh, that an old man should have such eyes! And the young such as I should fail to see!

ABRAHAM: O Isaac, be happy you do not see. Not yet. Be joyful that you have never talked with God. You have still small time for pleasure.

ISAAC: Still I do not see! Does the offering approach? Does he wing his way or run to us on eager legs?

ABRAHAM: He stands. He is still. He waits.

ISAAC: Why do we also wait? Let us take him and use him as God requires.

ABRAHAM: Hand me the rope.

ISAAC (BAFFLED): Here is the rope. Did you think I had not brought it? Did you doubt my obedience?

ABRAHAM (HIS VOICE BREAKING WITH EMOTION): No, that I did not. I know you as my fair and honest son who is ever obedient. Here. Give me your wrists.

ISAAC (SHOCKED REALISATION): You bind me! Father, you bind *me*!

ABRAHAM: I bind you as He binds me!

ISAAC: I? Am I then your sacrifice?

ABRAHAM: I would it were not so! I would... (PAUSE) But it *is* so. It is God's command. As you to me, so I to Him. He has command of me utterly.

BRIEF SILENCE

ISAAC: (RESIGNED NOW): Then it shall be. I could wish this cup pass from me. But to wish against the wish of God... (BEAT) Do it father, do it quickly.

ABRAHAM: I ask your forgiveness.

ISAAC: Only God can truly forgive. We are ever in His hands. (BEAT) Quickly! You have the knife! Do it quickly, I say!

TRUMPET

ANGEL:
Hold your hand, servant of the Lord!
For your obedience, mercy is your reward.
Throw down the knife upon the land,
Untie the bonds and let him stand
Unharmed, untroubled, much loved one,
Be pleased in him your blessed son!

THUNDERCLAP

GOD: My angel speaks well. Now listen to your God. (BEAT) Oh, I have tempted thee, Abraham. Haven't I just? (LAUGHS) Oh, I have tested thee! And I have tempted thee, young Isaac. Both to disobedience, the crime of your first parents. Now I lift the dread command of sacrifice. I leave you go in peace.

ANGEL:
This sacrifice need not be done.
But there is another son
who will be killed upon
an altar made to end the run
of Satan's power
in Satan's hour.

GOD: Enough of prophecy! They are saved for now. Let them take pleasure in the moment! It will be another father must face this dread deed on another day!

CRACKLE OF RADIO

SERIOUS MUSIC FADE UP, FADE DOWN THEN...

GOD: Hello, listeners. Hope you're still out there, still tuned in. This is the voice of God again. Listen to this!

THE SOUND OF A BEATING HEART

GOD (SPEAKING OVER IT): Hear that? That's my heart. I wanted you to know I have one too. I feel things like you do, but bigger, wider, so much more that I couldn't begin to describe it. Not in a way you'd understand right now. (BEAT) And now it's time for another new beginning. Yes. *Another* one. But no floods, no fire this time. I've decided to come down there, live with you a bit, find out what it's like first hand to be human. I mean, I know *exactly* what it's like already. Past and future all around me, inside me too. But sometimes you have to *do* a thing, not just think it. So you can *feel* it as well. Fathers and sons. Abraham and Isaac. What goes around comes around.

HEART STOPS

GOD: There. A heart-stopping moment. (BEAT) So. Whatever happens, you can take it from me that BBC Radio Universe will be covering it. What more can I say? Tune in tomorrow. Goodnight. God bless! And you can take *that* from *me*!

TRUMPETS.

CLOSING MUSIC, SAD AND DIGNIFIED

END

Also in Nettle Books: *Drama by Michael Yates*

The Bronte Boy

Branwell Bronte, who once ruled an imaginary world, is now a man, grown mad coping with the real one. As he slips down the road of drink and despair, his loving father Patrick and talented sister Charlotte make a last-ditch stand for his salvation, but Branwell's sinister friend, gravedigger John Brown, threatens to have the last word. (A performance of The Bronte Boy was commissioned by The Bronte Society for its AGM weekend in 2013.)
Paperback. 80 pages. £6. ISBN 978-0-9561513-1-5

Short Shorts Volume 1

Three one-act plays. *Life Sentence:* A vengeful wife pursues her faithless husband with an axe; *Till my Eyes Bleed:* Mel holds a wake for dead pal Adrian unaware of Adrian's relationship with Mel's wife; *Sunday Afternoon Again:* young Lenny worries about his parents fighting – and the wicked witch next door.
Paperback. 115 pages. £6. ISBN 978-0-9561513-3-9

Short Shorts Volume 2

Three one-act plays. *A Real Cushy Number:* It's night shift in the porters room at a major hospital and a death is on the cards; *All Good Men:* A leadership contest at the Labour Party conference mean the knives are out; *Luvvies:* A failed playwright and a bit-part actress ask a young couple back to their home for a night of drinks and ritual humiliation.
Paperback 136 pages. £6. ISBN 978-0-9561513-5-3

Also in Nettle Books

Flying with a Broken Wing
By Sat Mehta

Flying with a Broken Wing tells the true story of a boy growing up in India in turbulent times.

Sat Mehta was five years old when he and his family became refugees, caught up in the biggest migration in modern history at the time of Independence. His home was destroyed, his uncle murdered. Once very wealthy farmers, the Mehtas became destitute.

Later, Sat suffered a broken arm, complications set in and amputation seemed inevitable. As he lay in hospital, a world famous surgeon, Professor Robert Roaf, strode onto the ward, choosing "hopeless cases" to help. Sat got a second chance.

The gratitude he felt for the great man's skill shaped the rest of Sat's life. He qualified as a doctor and arrived in England, where he has lived and worked for 30 years.

He says of his life: "It is a story of a disappearing world, sadhus, snakes and baking sun, monkeys, monsoons and riot and murder. As a boy, I saw it all."

Paperback. 180 pages. £10. ISBN 978-0-9561513-2-2

www.ingramcontent.com/pod-product-compliance
Lightning Source LLC
Chambersburg PA
CBHW070537130626
46555CB00003B/1467